What Dwells between the Lines

WHAT DWELLS
BETWEEN THE LINES

Fifty-Three 53-Word Story Contest Winners
Plus Tips on Writing Remarkably Brief Fiction

Edited by
Kevin Morgan Watson
Claire V. Foxx
Christopher Forrest
Ella Watson

Press 53
Winston-Salem

Press 53, LLC
PO Box 30314
Winston-Salem, NC 27130

First Edition

Cover image by Maria Chaile,
acquired through Pexels.com

Cover design by Kevin Morgan Watson

Library of Congress Control Number
2024940172

ISBN 978-1-950413-81-2

Dedicated to
Mike Tuohy (1954-2021)
two-time winner of the
53-Word Story Contest

and to all the writers around the world
who have sent us their 53-word stories

Contents

Introduction

"What dwells between the lines" is the secret to writing great short fiction, especially remarkably brief fiction like a 53-word story. What isn't said in a story can speak volumes, and you'll find examples of that inside this book. Learning to tell your story in as few words as possible is difficult, but not impossible. It requires the ancient axiom known as Occam's Razor, which basically says, "Don't say with many words what can be said with a few."

We are believers in the idea that the shorter the art form, the more difficult it is to do well. Consider this six-word story, often attributed to Hemingway: "For sale: baby shoes, never worn." This is a wonderful example of "what dwells between the lines." Upon reading this story your mind immediately begins filling in the spaces creating a much larger story. Writing brief fiction is not easy, but that is the challenge. Write your story; then grab Occam's Razor and remove every word that is not necessary.

The free, monthly 53-Word Story Contest is about having fun, playing with language, and packing a big story into a small space. The way our contest works is simple: we offer a prompt on the first day of every month and writers have fifteen days to form a story using fifty-three words that surprises us. Hint: this can only be done by taking the prompt in a direction readers will not expect.

We want to thank all the teachers around the world who are using the 53-Word Story Contest in their classrooms. You'll find a few students in this collection who wowed us with their storytelling skills. Using the 53-Word Story Contest as a teaching tool is what inspired us to create this book of some of our favorite 53-word stories, along with a few tips from the pros on how to write remarkably brief fiction.

We hope you enjoy these stories. If you'd like to give our contest a try, the guidelines are at 53wordstory.com. It's free, it's fun, and you might win a book and publication of your story.

Give it a go. We want to read your 53-word story!

—The Editors

*What dwells between the lines
is essential in very short fiction.*

—Robert Scotellaro

Write a 53-word story about **a trip**

Open Road
by Jane Laube Boch

Mommy screamed when a truck drove by. It looked like Daddy's. But it wasn't, and we went back to putting our suitcases in the car. My backpack and teddy bear went up front with me. "Where are we going?" I asked.

Mommy revved the engine. "As far as my wallet will take us."

Note:
The 53-Word Story Contest began in 2011 as a fun challenge for Press 53's few-hundred email subscribers. We sent the winner a free book. Our first contest drew fewer than twenty entries.

Prompt for
December 2015

Write a 53-word story about **something slipping away**

Ancestry
by Mike Tuohy

A month after the stroke, Mama started getting names in the photo album right.

"That's Reverend Kelso with Mr. Echols, holding the beagle. There's your daddy and Mrs. Tate. She had the diabetes."

"Hold on, Mama. That's Dr. Stotts, not Daddy."

Seeing her horrified expression, I felt half of my ancestry slip away.

Note:
In the early stages of the contest, our prompts could be quite specific: "Write a 53-word story about the last coconut on the island." We eventually began offering the prompt with a simple sentence to give the writer more room to create.

Prompt for
August 2016

August is here, and I don't know about you, but I'm ready for autumn. Cooler days, windows open at night, that crisp feeling in the air. Until then, we'll have to stay cool and try not to melt. Which brings me to our prompt for this month.

Write a 53-word story about **something melting**

Gettysburg, July, 1863
by Theresa Wyatt

One soldier took a bullet which shattered his femur. The next day he woke up in a cellar with a woman leaning over him picking wax from his beard. She apologized, said the doctor needed light to amputate in the dark. Candles melted down to nothing were stuck everywhere, even in her bonnet.

Note:
"Gettysburg, July, 1863" was selected for inclusion in *NEW MICRO: Exceptionally Short Fiction,* published by W. W. Norton & Company, Inc., 2018, edited by James Thomas and Robert Scotellaro. This story was also a finalist for *Best Small Fictions 2017*, published by Braddock Avenue Books, Series Editor, Tara Lynn Masih; Guest Editor, Amy Hempel.

November already? Ahead of us are the holidays: Thanksgiving and then Christmas. A time for gatherings, family, friends, food, and hopefully fun times. Lots of activity and, if we're lucky, some down-time. On any given day, someone stirs in the kitchen, while someone stirs from a nap because someone is stirring up trouble.

Write a 53-word story about **stirring**

Nine O'Clock Evening News
by Laura Hunter

"Don't be stirring me up now."

"I'm not meaning to, Mama. I'm needing to tell you something."

"You slammed that door again. Turn and face the corner."

"But this is important."

"Nothing more important than doing what I say."

The kitchen light flickered.

Carol cried, "Daddy's in the barn, stobbed by the bull!"

Note:
In November 2016, we began the tradition of a 53-word introduction to the prompt, an idea by Press 53 volunteer Michael Mount. Why didn't we think of that? Thank you, Michael!

Happy New Year from everyone at *Prime Number Magazine* and Press 53! For luck, health, and prosperity in the New Year, be sure to place a penny under your plate at dinner. And while you are at it, think about how you will go about writing your first 53-word story for the year.

Write a 53-word story about **a penny**

Fair Trade
by Claire V. Foxx

"Some rock" was his initial appraisal.

"I always thought so," she said.

He inspected the ring, reached into his mustache for a real number. "Tough break. Give you 350."

"How much for that?" She pointed to one of a dozen revolvers shelved under the glass countertop.

"349.99?"

"That's a deal. Keep the change."

Note:
Claire worked for Press 53 as a volunteer editor the summer of 2018 between her junior and senior years of college. She is now Press 53 Short Fiction Editor (she is also a brilliant cover designer—an art major turned English major).

When June rolls around, many of us think "Break time!" We take a break from work or school to travel, we cross fingers for a break in the weather, and hope no summer activities lead to broken bones, broken windows, or broken hearts. From time to time, we all need a nice break.

Write a 53-word story about **a break**

How Amelia Earhart Comes to Understand Gravitational Pull
by Joanna Thomas

To the roof of the shed, she cobbles a ramp, then rides an apple crate down the slope. The wooden box splinters upon impact. Split lip, ripped bloomers, and a snoot full of exhilaration, she exclaims, "Oh, Pidge, it's just like flying!" Later, over the Pacific, the flap, flutter, thrill of another plummet.

Note:
The rule ignored most by participants of our contest is: "NO ATTACHEMNTS! Please paste your story into the body of your email." When you are reading hundreds of 53-word stories, opening an attachment can double the time it takes.

March is here and with it comes St. Paddy's Day, not to be confused with St. Patty's Day, which doesn't even exist. We've all heard of the luck of the Irish, which came about in the late 1800s when many successful gold miners happened to be Irish. Irish or not, good luck, writer.

Write a 53-word story about **luck**

Might Get Lucky
by Anne Anthony

"Just my luck," she whispered to Jane sitting at the bar.
"They like their mothers," Jane whispered back.
"Listen, you might get lucky. When's the last time . . ."
"Shut up."
She swallowed her third shot of bourbon, and considered her options.
"Mrs. Kelly?" He flashed a familiar grin. "Bobby. Remember? You were my babysitter."

Writing tip

When space is at a premium—and it always is—pay attention to the length and cadence of your sentences. Crafting a meter and flow that align with your intent will maximize the effectiveness of your language. Move us along; slow us down. Don't be afraid of a little poetry in your prose. —Christopher Forrest, Press 53 Poetry Editor

Prompt for
April 2018

April is National Poetry Month, a time to celebrate language, our senses and sensibilities, our ability to communicate ideas and emotions in a peaceful way. A poem can be found, experienced, lived, or witnessed in all manner of ways. Poets look at the obvious and make us see it in an unexpected way.

Write a 53-word story about **a poem**

Hailstones
by Laura Ruth Loomis

"It's so vivid." Jason pointed to the passage where Joanna described her father's fists coming down like the hailstones that left permanent dents in the hood of the old pickup. The way the hail had burned against her cheeks. "I wish I could write like you."

"No," Joanna said quietly. "You really don't."

Prompt for
June 2018

June 14 is Flag Day: a patriotic commemoration. June 21 is the summer solstice: an observance of cosmic proportions. But on June 29, International Mud Day celebrates that humblest mixture of water and earth. Mud soils and stains. Mud oozes, erodes, and fertilizes. Mud makes excellent facials. We hope it inspires great fiction.

Write a 53-word story about **mud**

Low Tide
by Annie Dodson

Every morning, she walked down to the muddy shore, searching for footprints. The events of the previous night were revealed, the wildlife rush-hour report. The fox's dainty prints, barely visible, the ominous alligator slides, the hand-like prints of the mother raccoon with two kits in tow. Her heart sank—yesterday, there were three.

Writing tip
A flash fiction should be like a helicopter, not an airplane; it should go straight up without any runway. (Easier said than done, of course.) —David Jauss, author of *Alone with All That Could Happen: On Writing Fiction*

National Lemon Juice Day is August 29. We'll drink to that—make it a tall glass of fresh-squeezed, sweet-and-sour lemonade. But if you've ever had a sour mood, seen a sour face, heard a sour note, or misread the expiration date on a carton of milk, you know not everything sour is so refreshing.

Write a 53-word story about **something sour**

Nuptials
by Emily West

They were married at a state park in Texas, where thunderstorms had driven the rattlesnakes out of their dens. Poison ivy rashes raged under his tuxedo and the blisters on his finger burst and oozed when they exchanged rings. They drank whiskey sours at the reception and pretended not to believe in omens.

Writing tip

Maybe you start with an establishing shot, zoomed out, a little terse, and just hinting at the mood. You move the camera closer, and find a prop to do some heavy lifting. Then, with ten or twelve words left, a close-up gets you to the emotion and the why of the story. —Emily West

Prompt for
September 2018

Autumn is coming. Cooler weather, the foliage will change color, and the temperature begins to fall. Fall is another name for our third season, from the Old English word "feallan," meaning "to fall or to die," inspired, no doubt, by the falling leaves or from people falling all over themselves to get outside.

Write a 53-word story about **a fall**

Taking the Fall
by Mike Tuohy

My father pointed and gave me the look. "I told you he was gone next time it happened."

It was a big pile. Max was a big dog.

"It wasn't Max. It was me." I braced for the slap.

My father sighed. "Maybe it's time you learned how to build a dog pen."

Writing tip

To be a writer is to be a decision-maker. As you draft your sentences, what decisions are you making about your character's desire? What decisions are you making about obstacles to that desire? What circumstances can you imagine that will allow your character's innermost yearning to shine forth? A story is simply this: Someone wants. . . . But. . . . So. . . . Then. —Katey Schultz, author of *Flashes of War* and *Still Come Home*

Prompt for
April 2019

Who in the history of literature would you choose to eat dinner with tonight, were they still alive? The author of this month's winning story may choose up to five writers that *Prime Number Magazine* will arrange to have resurrected for a private dinner on the planet Tralfamadore. Kurt Vonnegut will be there.

Write a 53-word story about **foolishness**

Guts
by Brian Rosten

Amanda leaned over the bell tower railing. Grass flailed in the wind as if to say "don't do it."

She glanced at Victor, her face a pale orange against the sunrise. "I can't," she finally admitted.

He lifted the chum, visibly disappointed as he rained fish guts down onto an unsuspecting Associate Dean.

Writing tip
Choose dynamic verbs to convey the action in a story. Rather than relying on adverbs or adjectives, substitute a verb in their place. For example, eliminate adverbs by turning "she ran very quickly" into "she raced" to reduce your word count. Likewise drop adjectives—"It was a dark and stormy night" becomes "The night raged." Verb choice is key when writing tiny stories. —Anne Anthony, "Might Get Lucky," (March 2018)

Every four years in the U.S., the first Tuesday in November is Election Day. Citizens weigh their options, form their opinions, and cast their votes: Right or Left? For or against? The decision is never unanimous. But that's the name of the game: the will of (most of) the people. Survey says . . .

Write a 53-word story about **a majority**

Alone
by Jane T. Pait

Papa, babysitting two-year-old triplets, took a bathroom break. He heard the sound of the toy box being pushed down the hall and stopping by the bathroom door. Giggling, then the ominous click of the deadbolt installed to keep the girls from playing in the commode, and three sets of tiny feet running away.

Writing tip

Write the story and do not worry about word count or typos. Then when your ideas are on paper/in PC, remove all unnecessary wording and correct the typos. This way, you will not interrupt the creative flow of the story.
—Jane T. Pait

December 2019

In December 1620, 102 Pilgrim settlers arrived from Europe in present-day Massachusetts, ready for a fresh start in the so-called "new world." Everything was different: the land; the people; the food (or lack thereof); the illnesses; the long, brutal winter. Plymouth put the "New" in "New England"—but new doesn't always mean better . . .

Write a 53-word story about **something new**

Good Night
by Brian Rosten

Dr. Manecilla smiled as the mouse's eyes drooped. It had been another big day for the genetically spliced rodent. Dr. Manecilla had run Skippy through a battery of tests to prove handedness was hereditary. Another day; still no side effects.

"Good night," the doctor said, turning out the lights.
"Good night," Skippy replied.

Writing tip
Think of the prompt as a house. Walk in the front door and look around, but don't start writing just yet; visit the other rooms, peek into the closets, open some drawers, check out the attic, the garage, the basement. There are other stories, better stories, hiding in plain sight. Take some time to find them. —The Editors

For some of us, this season of resolution is one of deprivations. Detrimental foodstuffs will linger on shelves; other vices will be left wanting. We will nurture an unfilled space within our mass. Incidentally, this month in 1875 George Green patented the first electric dental drill. Behold the convergence of unfulfillment and decay.

Write a 53-word story about **a cavity**

Breakaway
by Scott B. Shepherd

JoJo peers out warily. Maybe she's napping; maybe she's waiting for him. He can't hide in the couch forever. One chance. Deep breath. He leaps. Tiny claws catch in the carpet. He's doomed.

"Hamster!" Chloe shrieks as she pounces. "Just in time for tea!"

Here comes a doll dress. There goes JoJo's dignity.

Writing tip
Picture a Norman Rockwell painting. A child outside the principal's office wearing a black eye and a wide smile. We can see the story. Approach your story the same way by freezing a moment in your mind; then look around for details that tell the story. Write more than you need and then whittle it down to its essence, leaving only what is necessary. —Scott B. Shepherd

Prompt for
February 2020

This month, the Kansas City Chiefs return to the Super Bowl after a fifty-year run of coming up short. Vegas will run the numbers and the 49ers will run the ball. Many expect the Chiefs to run the table. In this spirit, let's run with the word that has the most dictionary definitions.

Write a 53-word story about **a run**

Endurance
by Elizabeth Barton

Arm outstretched, she searched for the perfect spot on the rear bumper. She'd made the sticker herself—bold digits 1079 against blue sky and cottony clouds. She'd get questions. Everyone understood what 26.2 meant, but how many people knew the page total for *Infinite Jest*? She'd inform them. It had been her marathon.

Writing tip
You've surely heard the writing advice write what you know. This might make sense if you're writing, say, a book about architecture or an essay about geopolitics; but for writers of fiction, curiosity is our superpower. I think it's far more interesting to write what you want to know. Find the topic that ignites your curiosity, do the research or the soul-searching, and THEN write what you know.
—Christopher Allen, publisher of *SmokeLong Quarterly*

Prompt for
July 2020

This year, our vacations (or staycations) may look different. But we can dream, can't we? Imagine: sunrise on the shore, miles of cool sand, shells endlessly polished by the tide. Strangely collectible, these bony souvenirs: proof, in every color, that there's always room to grow. Or is it "there's no place like home"?

Write a 53-word story about **a shell**

And All the Heavens Are in Disarray
by Kristin Tenor

Late at night they lie side by side counting tiny holes scattered like a constellation across the ceiling tiles above her hospital bed—big bear, little bear, an arrow aimed towards Cancer who has escaped its crab-like carapace and will not go back. He kisses her temple wishing they were by the sea.

Writing tip
Resonance is often considered the gold standard to any lasting piece of literature. That's why when writing very short fiction it's vital to consider the duality and emotional weight the details carry. For instance, the word "Cancer" not only names the well-known constellation, but could also infer a diagnosis. This inference invites the reader to tap into their own experiences and/or emotions, building a connection that may generate an empathic response towards the character. —Kristin Tenor

Prompt for
August 2020

"August is the Sunday of summer," or so they say. One season ends, and another begins. Sunday is sabbath, to some: a day of rest and reflection for the week ahead. To others, it's a day of worldly pleasures: sleeping late, taking a break from the nine-to-five grind. Of course, Monday always awaits . . .

Write a 53-word story about **a Sunday**

Lazy Sunday
by Riddhishrree Badhan

At eight in the morning, her alarm went off. She reluctantly opened her eyes, then closed them again. Seconds later, she stood with resolve. Avoiding the enticing trap, she brushed, showered, and finished breakfast. I've finally done it! she thought gleefully, turning towards her desk. Then, at twelve noon, her eyes slowly opened.

Writing tip

Begin your story as close to the end as possible, use action and dialogue that makes the reader curious, and surprise the reader with your ending. Just write; then look for words that don't add anything to the story and cut them. ~~Only~~ use ~~strong~~ words that ~~will~~ inform the reader and move the story forward. —Kevin Morgan Watson, Press 53 Publisher & Editor in Chief

Prompt for
September 2020

September has nine of the ten most-common birthdates for Americans (September 9 being the nation's most popular). As summer becomes autumn, and nature takes a turn for dry and dark, abundant new life brings much-needed hope. Diapers and 2 a.m. wake-up calls. And toothless grins that make it all worthwhile . . .

Write a 53-word story about **a birth**

Premature Congratulations
by N.E. Rule

"Ridiculous to have let a pregnant woman on board," the nurse chides while clearing the mucus from the tiny baby's mouth.

"Her due date wasn't for six more weeks, and she's the Captain's friend." The doctor winks then the baby wails. "That's encouraging," he says swaddling it in white linen stamped *RMS Titanic*.

Writing tip

Don't explain everything. Mystery is not a virtue in and of itself—but every great story has a certain mysteriousness about it, something ineffable and curious that leaves us wondering. Instead of telling the reader what it all means, great fiction asks, "What does it all mean?" Loose ends are sometimes the best part. —Claire V. Foxx, Press 53 Short Fiction Editor

This month at Press 53 we are feeling grateful: we celebrated our fifteenth anniversary in October; we created our very first 500-piece limited-edition jigsaw puzzle to celebrate; we launched our largest issue ever of *Prime Number Magazine* and hosted our first online reading with contributors. So we must say to everyone, Thank you!

Write a 53-word story about **thanks**

Buy a Donkey
by Jean-Luke Swanepoel

The last thing the self-help presenter had said was buy a donkey. So Irma bought a donkey. The presenter, being South African, had in fact said *baie dankie*, Afrikaans for "thank you very much," but Irma found the donkey to be an excellent listener, and urged her friends to buy donkeys as well.

Writing tip
Dive right in. Write it down. Put it aside. Let it simmer till it cools. Bring it out and fix it. Repeat as necessary. Don't wait for inspiration. Inspiration is nice if you're lucky enough to be embraced by the muse, but the essence of writing is revision, and lots of it. —Dennis McFadden, author of *Jimtown Road*, winner of the 2016 Press 53 Award for Short Fiction

Prompt for
December 2020

Today, December 1, is National Giving Day, when people are encouraged to give to their favorite charity or business. But we think it should also mean giving to someone you love or giving someone another chance. We give all the time: we give up, give back, give a hoot, and give a hand.

Write a 53-word story about **giving**

The Signs
by Jo Mularczyk

A woman's scream rent the air. "The lake is boiling!"

"Father these portents warn me not to marry," Helena entreated. Her betrothed was old and cruel.

"Nonsense, daughter."

A bird fell beside them, dead.

"By the Gods, Father, read the signs!"

"Enough! Today I give you to the richest man in all Pompeii."

Note:
In 2020, the 53-Word Story Contest received a total of 13,906 stories from writers around the world. One month alone we received 1,757.

Tapping a keg of beer can take some practice. Writing a story usually requires a revision or two. On six different occasions the United States employed military conscription. Many bills are deducted automatically from our bank accounts. Cyclists utilize aerodynamics via slipstream. Horses. Is it cold in here? I thought I felt something.

Write a 53-word story about **a draft**

What She's Having
by Rachel Jager

Sinking into a barstool, her body deflated under the shoulder pads that suddenly made her feel like she was playing dress-up in her father's closet. Replaying scenes from the boardroom, she cursed her indecision and swore that she was done going with the flow.

"What'll it be?"

"Whatever is on tap is fine."

Writing tip
Don't tell me the moon is shining; show me the glint of light on broken glass. —Anton Chekhov

The Ides of March is familiar. Beware! However, "ides" does not come up that often elsewhere. That makes it a fossil word: in use thanks to a particular phrase, but otherwise obsolete. Ides is kith and kin with "petard," "druthers," and, well, "kith"—relegated to the dusty files of lingual archaeologists. Good "riddance"?

Without further "ado," write a 53-word story about **fossils**

Underground Fugitive
by Ada Young

My leader's cloaked form staggered as we fled. Cries pierced the air. The barrel of a gun flashed. The doors of the safehouse were boarded, shielding the terror.

The babe I swaddled was numbingly cold.

The ground found us, accepted us, held us close. The world takes lives, but the earth keeps them.

Note:
Ada was in seventh grade when she wrote "Underground Fugitive."

Prompt for
April 2021

Fools are known for their imprudence. They may suffer from harmless derangement. They may be a court jester. *Merriam-Webster* informs that a fool is also a cold dessert of pureed fruit with whipped cream. So, if someone says, "I ate a delicious fool last night," be careful, but they probably just mean parfait.

Write a 53-word story about **something tasty**

That Awkward First Kiss
by Paul Adam Short

My mouth tingles from the grape ChapStick smudge her lips have pressed on to mine. She thinks I'm blushing as I cover my face. My throat's closed. I scramble in my backpack for the EpiPen. I wonder if her sandwich was PB & J.

My chemical savior plunges into skin. Now I'm blushing.

Writing tip
Make no mistake, clichés hang on a story like a cheap suit, so avoid them like the plague. —Kevin Morgan Watson, Press 53 Publisher & Editor in Chief

William Faulkner once avoided the period for more than 1,200 straight words. Jonathan Coe put off using one for nearly 14,000. There are entire books, in myriad languages and genres, containing only a single period. Each author understood their own unique motivation, but perhaps they all regarded it as a little dot prison.

Write a 53-word story about **a sentence**

What Defines You
by Angel Pritts

It was her third time caught stealing. "Your choice," sighed the judge.

A month in jail or a day holding a sign: I AM A THIEF. Obvious decision.

People stared, laughed. A stranger approached her, pointing at her sign. "That doesn't define you."

She cried; they hugged. He never did find his wallet.

Writing tip
Write toward "sticking the landing." A good flash does something, twists something, reveals something, in the final line. This genre is not about compressing a longer story; it's more like a Rubik's Cube reveal—complex, sometimes twisted, and fits into the palm of your hand. Write the title knowing it's an opportunity for a sneak peak, a moral, or its own micro-micro fiction, and have fun! —Kate Hill Cantrill, author of *Walk Back from Monkey School*

Prompt for
June 2021

Whistling is hard to teach. It usually goes: "Just make a circle with your lips and blow." And soon after, "Yeah, kinda." Whistles, themselves, are easier. June celebrates milk, bourbon, smoothies, moonshine, iced tea, martinis, rosé, the Dark 'N' Stormy, cider, and general hydration, so there's plenty of occasion to wet yours. Poo-tee-weet?

Write a 53-word story about **a whistle**

I Can Do It with My Eyes Shut
by Audrey Lindsay

My other collie whines as I pay the vet.

"Hush, Bessie's coming home!" Infection has turned her eyes milky.

Back at the farm, she pads, unseeing, a working dog no longer.

Next morning, in the far field, I whistle. "Come bye."

The flock suddenly bleats and swerves.

Tail wagging, Bessie has found us.

Writing tip
Every character should want something, even if it is only a glass of water. —Kurt Vonnegut, Jr.

July's birthstone is the ruby. "Ruby" comes from the Latin word *ruber*, meaning "red." If you add the letter *b*, we get "rubber," which is named for being efficient at rubbing off pencil marks. "Pencil" rhymes with "tinsel" and some people celebrate Christmas in July. What was I saying? I've gotten off track.

Write a 53-word story about **a train**

The Buzz about the Wedding
by Greg Hill

As the groom speaks haltingly but lovingly at the outdoor reception, everyone assumes the tears which bedew the radiant cheeks of his bride's smiling yet stoic face reveal her elation, not realizing the train of her dress has disturbed a nest of ground hornets, now assaulting her legs, trapped below layers of tulle.

Writing tip
Often, general advice to writers is to begin from a reference point of "what you know." I would simply flip this idea and support an additional approach which would encourage exploring, researching, and writing from a place of "what you *don't* know." —Theresa Wyatt, "Gettysburg, July, 1863" (August 2016)

Prompt for
August 2021

There is a little jellyfish that is effectively immortal thanks to their ability to transform their own cells. Bananas have no such talent. We seem somewhere in between. Statistically, the month of August tends to capture the most human births. Some 9% of you will add a candle to your cake this month.

Write a 53-word story about **ripening**

Ship Seeking Ship
by Hayley Igarashi

"We were like two trains passing in the night," Fiona told her sister. This was after their first bottle of pinot, but before karaoke.

"*Ships* pass in the night," Mabel said.

Fiona imagined lovers bobbing by on wine-red waves, instead of barreling through on immutable tracks.

"Well," Fiona said, "that explains a lot."

Note:
In the summer of 2023, the 53-Word Story Contest was featured in *Breathe* magazine (UK) in an article titled, "Miniature Joys," by Stephanie Lam, which included four 53-word stories: "He Never Asked Me What I Wanted" by Madeleine McDonald; "Final Request" by Keith Padraic; "Unforgettable" by Janette Ostle; and "Ship Seeking Ship" by Hayley Igarashi.

Oyez! Oyez! Oyez! After August comes September. That's important to agree upon for any calendar arrangements. The 53-Word Society accepts stories through September 15, written by *homo sapiens* (see taxonomic rank). Content remains at the sole discretion of the author. Create your own menu, so to speak. Now, go forth, write, and submit!

Write a 53-word story about **an order**

Equine Knocks
by Sandra Burley

It is hot, humid August, the smell abominable. The debate on horse-drawn tourist carts had raged throughout Spring. Being a tourist guide in Charleston, I was undecided. Money was tight. We needed the business. But the poor horses! In the end, the activists won. Hoisting the handles of my rickshaw, I began trotting.

Writing tip
Listen to the voice inside your head as if it was your boss. It is. Start writing as if you're taking dictation. If you can, close your eyes and type, ignoring punctuation and typos. Fix them later. Get that voice now—words, rhythm, rhyme—before the voice starts talking to someone who listens. —Sandra Burley

October 2021

October brings to mind long drives, harvest time, full moons, changing colors, falling leaves, Halloween, and beer. Did you know that at the end of Oktoberfest in Munich, everyone holds hands and sings John Denver's "County Roads"? It could be true. Maybe that was a one-off? One thing is certain: October is here.

Write a 53-word story about **arriving**

Final Request
by Keith Padraic

I left Santorini by boat, traveled to Athens by motorbike. I flew to Queens, then Boston, arriving with sand in my hair. My relatives parted like the sea as I knelt by my grandfather. I held the conch to his ear, and he listened to the shores of his youth one last time.

Writing tip
Write without regard to word-count, later eliminating wherever possible to reach length requirements. Employ contractions, creative punctuation, phrases and fragments to reduce bloat. Sacrifice those 'darling' sentences that (although inspire fondness) do not serve the whole; and be open to new directions not originally conceived of, allowing for the story to surprise you. —Keith Padraic

Prompt for
November 2021

Pillows have come a long way. You can find pillows of down, feather, memory foam, Poly-Fil, buckwheat hull, microbead, wool, and much else. Some hotels have pillow menus for discerning sleepers. Not bad for a device that got its start, in part, by keeping bugs out of our hair, mouths, noses, and ears.

Write a 53-word story about **support**

Unforgettable
by Janette Ostle

He rocks by the window, watches rain slip down the pane. There's nothing else, his reflection blurred a long time ago.

Standing beside him, she lets the stylus fall, hums the tune, sings the words, offers her hand.

"Shall we?"

And while they dance to their song, he is fluid in the present.

Writing tip
Think small in scope, but big in concept. So much epiphany and wonder can be explored in something as simple as the act of washing the dishes. Novelists go out into their world and explore all the paths, but flash fiction writers can't afford that luxury—we have to pick one smooth stone and peer closely seeing the entire world in its reflection.
—Tara Laskowski, author of *The Weekend Retreat*

Aladdin had three wishes. Goldilocks had three beds, chairs, porridge bowls—but some of the best things in life come in pairs. From twins to turtle doves (as the carolers sing), two's company. Who's Batman without Robin? Harry Nilsson says "Two can be as bad as one . . ." but hopefully 2022 is twice as nice.

Write a 53-word story about **a dynamic duo**

Craving for Two
by Nina Miller

There's not enough malt vinegar in the world to quench my desire for battered haddock nestled in a mound of greasy chips wrapped in oil-soaked newspaper.

"There's a chip shop open somewhere," hubby insists, blinded by the rising sun.

I feel the boys wrestle in utero, hoping to calm them with crispy filet.

Writing Tip
Never use a metaphor, simile, or other figure of speech which you are used to seeing in print. —George Orwell

Prompt for
February 2022

In 1872, the English poet Christina Rossetti wrote of the traditional bleak midwinter, when "Snow had fallen, snow on snow, / Snow on snow . . ." through a moaning frosty wind to an iron-hard earth. In 2022, a search engine will return a superabundance of recipes for homemade snow ice cream in less than a second.

Write a 53-word story about **being resourceful**

Please Follow Proper Courtroom Etiquette
by Sara Elizabeth (Elle) Dowd

The witness testimony is crucial, filling the interpreter's brain with dovetailing streams of letters, concepts, and possible renderings. All eyes lock on her as the silence awaiting her interpretation threatens to swallow her whole.

Rummaging quickly through her arsenal of Korean slang, she locates the equivalent in English. Satisfied, she begins:

"That shithead . . ."

Writing tip

Learn proper punctuation. In U.S. literature, for example, commas and periods are never placed outside the quotation marks. "Never." Placing them outside is a British rule. Editors love working with writers who know the rules.
—The Editors

Prompt for
March 2022

An anagrammatist might say that spring is the *charm* of March. They might say that our third month of March holds a special place in their heart (specifically *atriums*) being named after the first month of the Roman calendar, "Martius." A Pisces grows *spices*. An Aries watches the daffodils *arise* from the dirt.

Write a 53-word story about **rearranging**

Don't Mess with Dewey
by Jill Mills

Meg stared at the clash of colors lining the walls. To her eyes this was chaos to be tamed. As she worked, a smooth gradient appeared from red to violet . . . a perfect rainbow. "MEG!" came a harsh whisper, breaking the pleasure of the moment. "What have you done? . . . The books . . ." sighed the librarian.

Writing tip
Never use an adverb to modify the verb "said."
—Elmore Leonard ~~wisely~~ said

Prompt for
April 2022

Hubble telescope glimpsed a star they named Earandel, meaning "morning star," whose light took 12.9 billion years to reach Earth. If the universe is 100, the Earandel we see is from when the universe was seven. However you go about trying to consider these enormities, it's hard not to be romantic about starlight.

Write a 53-word story about **a date**

Dusk
by H.T. Grossen

Harold's arthritic fingers straightened his tie.

Outside, Geraldine tended her flowers. She always loved gardening; but the sun was dropping quickly, and mother would soon call her in to dinner.

A dapper older man approached, carrying a tray of lemonade and sandwiches. He smiled.

Recognition flickered in hollow baby-blues.

"Happy Fiftieth Anniversary, darling."

Writing tip
When writing from a prompt, you need to think outside the box. Way outside. No, further. Other people have already thought of that! Originality is a big piece of the writing puzzle. Another piece is Titles: as important as they are difficult. A good title will not only compliment the writing it will also reveal something about the piece.
—H.T. Grossen

Prompt for
July 2022

The most famous "Julius" two thousand years ago was Caesar. The most famous one now might be Orange. An Orange Julius is made from egg whites, ice, orange concentrate, milk, vanilla, and sugar. Julius Caesar's ingredients are a bit more complicated. But, by name or by heat, we appreciate them both in July.

Write a 53-word story about **a connection**

Leaving Kyiv
by Carrie Keyes

Lydia stares out the train window at Vanko. He stands on the platform, his hand on the pane. The train rolls forward; she turns to watch him wave.

After she crosses into Poland, one thing remains: the loops and whorls of his fingerprints on the glass, lingering like a ghost longing to stay.

Writing tip

Lead with visible action and motion. Let the ideas swirl in its wake and drift outwardly. Leave a little mystery behind. Your reader is a passenger in your story; he/she wants to travel with you on the same, yet individual journey. —Carrie Keyes

A lot gets negotiated in August. We might get bids on inside projects. Laminate or granite? We might negotiate extra time at our favorite diner or bar. We might negotiate belt loops. We might get a negotiating headache and take non-prescription pharmaceuticals for relief. All just possibilities—perhaps you have a better proposal?

Write a 53-word story about **a counter**

The Last Word
by Beverley Ward

While other men fought about real estate, he didn't fight at all. But, at Christmas, the fairy was missing a wing. At Easter, decapitated simnel chickens lined the cake box. When my lover opened Monopoly, the top hat was gone. He even took the Z from Scrabble. He always had the last word.

Writing tip
Every story is a tightrope act that captures a moment of everlasting internal change. That change may be contained in the decision to take the first step onto the wire, the relief of the last step of the crossing, or the uncertainty that rises when a sudden gust catches the vulnerable walker unawares. —Clint McCown, author of *Mr. Potato Head vs. Freud: Lessons on the Craft of Writing Fiction*.

Prompt for
September 2022

Thirty days has September. Like the day count, plenty starts to fall this month. Trees begin shedding their leaves and temperatures often tumble. Chips descend into beans and cheeses and guacamoles and salsas and myriad other layers. And if you need a reminder, September is in that little trough beside your pinky knuckle.

Write a 53-word story about **a dip**

Lucky
by Zoë Jones

Fingers registered plastic and pulled an army man from the prize bag. Tiny gun clutched, legs crouched, green like grass. Luck's gift, a faceless totem. Toy came home, found a shrine on bed's empty pillow. I wrapped him in clay and whispered soft spells, casting my kismet to another soldier buried in sand.

Writing tip

Try to convey an emotion to the reader rather than a specific plot. If the reader is able to empathize with the story and its emotions, it may leave a stronger imprint. The exact plot can be left to the reader so they will connect with the story in their own personal way. —Zoë Jones

The remarkable pumpkin is not only both gourd and squash, but also, technically, a fruit. We celebrate the gourd with decorations on stoops and kitchen tables. We dress up the squash with nutmeg, pie crust, and whipped cream. The fruit owes to the seeds, often found steaming in the oven awaiting coarse salt.

Write a 53-word story about **potential**

Sourdough
by Jordan Hua

Resting precariously on the dryer of my laundry room, next to the heater. In a few hours it could completely transform. Change in form, texture, taste. Rise dramatically like a balloon. Turn golden, flour dusted, soft, airy, and slightly astringent. It could, couldn't it? It said four teaspoons, not *tablespoons*, right? Hold on—

Note:
Jordan was thirteen years old when she wrote "Sourdough."

Prompt for
November 2022

In California's Redwood National Forest lives 380-foot Hyperion. Nearby are Helios and Icarus, Hyperion's towering, yet shorter siblings. Each of their names evoke the sun toward which they stretch. Reared by its light and a dependent rain, protected now in their vulnerable seniority by park superintendents. How proud all the parents must be.

Write a 53-word story about **a tree**

He Never Asked Me What I Wanted
by Madeleine McDonald

Zeus granted my husband's wish, in return for our hospitality to an unknown traveler. We are oak and linden now, deep rooted, our branches intertwined. Yet my husband made that impulsive, sentimental request for death not to separate us. Me, I would have asked for the well not to run dry in summer.

Writing tip
When writing micro-fiction, start with everything you want to say, then pare back to the required length. Slowly. Over several versions. —Madeleine McDonald

Prompt for
December 2022

"December" comes from the Romantic combination of the Italian *dici*, meaning "to say," and the English *ember*, referring to a live piece of a dying fire. This etymology, of course, aligns perfectly with the month that ends our year. Even more of course is that this is all totally made up and untrue.

Write a 53-word story about **nonsense**

Ineptias Verba
by Sheri Holden-Peck

Time traveling has its perks and challenges. I was stuck in 1692 once. When the Reverend Parris fell, I performed basic first aid and saved his leg. I should've kept my mouth shut instead of intoning faux Latin for a sense of gravitas. Luckily, I was picked up before the bonfire was ready.

Writing tip
Use plain, simple language, short words and brief sentences. That is the way to write . . . stick to it; don't let fluff and flowers and verbosity creep in. —Mark Twain

Prompt for
January 2023

To many, a new year brings resolutions of productivity, diet, self-care, accumulation, giving, travel, time with family, and myriad others. If you need an early reminder from the universe that there's room to fall short and indulge every now and again, the chemical compound that gives nacho cheese its lovely gooeyness is $Na_3C_6H_5O_7$.

Write a 53-word story about **balance**

Round and Round
by Amanda Van Regenmorter

The fool, complexion mottled and clothing garish, cartwheeled round the court.

"Seas rise, mountains crumble, and I tell the tale!" he sing-songed. Titters followed. "Lords and ladies play cats and dogs whilst the king's away, but it's the queen in heat."

Silence fell as the queen withdrew her hand from the ambassador's arm.

Writing tip
Sometimes ideas don't need to be definitively fleshed out on the page because the communication happening between reader and writer is based on inference, resonance, and association. Be intentional with your words, but then release them and trust that they will be received.
—Tara Campbell, author and teacher

We can credit Roman calendar development around the Lunar Year for this shortened period called February. This month, for many, is a difficult one marked by hard weather and taxing conditions. Our resident cowboy poet posited, "When they were determining the months, they took days away from this one out of sheer dread."

Write a 53-word story about **grit**

Walk a Mile
by Sue McMillan

She thinks it's pebbles in her sock, then remembers she's not wearing socks. She takes off her right shoe, shakes it out. Like a finger puppet, her thumb pokes through the hole in the sole, waggling at her.

She crosses out "Anything" from "Anything Helps" on her cardboard sign and writes "Right Shoe."

Writing tip

The difficulty sometimes in revising a piece is getting the necessary distance to make it unfamiliar. Time helps, but that's not always possible (and writers tend to be impatient). One simple, yet effective, trick is to change the font. You literally will see the writing in a way that you didn't before. —Joseph Mills, author of *Bleachers: Fifty-Four Linked Fictions*

The season of spring returns in March and with it, perhaps, allergies. It seems a paradox to say "not to get your dander up," but that phrase stems from baking and brewing, and it means "try not to get too frothy." Brewing tea should be fine, though; the March Hare always thinks so.

Write a 53-word story about **madness**

Ergot
by Deborah Block-Schwenk

"'Twas the grain! Not the devil!" Prudence stood in the entrance to the barn, a knife in her shaking hands. "Look," she screamed.

The farmers crowded in. The torn-open bag of rye revealed tiny purple digits strewn among the grains.

"She's bewitched the harvest, too."

They dragged her screaming down to the water.

Writing tip
Make sure your title works hard. It can establish setting, characters, or foreshadow tone. By offering concrete, quirky details like the specific name of a character or street or grocery store, the title can immediately draw in your reader. A longer title on a brief piece creates a delicious moment of unexpected contrast. —Kathleen McGookey, author of *Paper Sky: Prose Poems*

Archaeologists say that humans developed agriculture and pottery many millennia before the invention of the wheel. Now, when many people by a stroke of their thumb can have groceries delivered in an hour, it's hard to comprehend eight thousand years of producing heavy things to be carried or dragged; moved only by burden.

Write a 53-word story about **sweat**

The End of the World as We Know It
by A.K. Murphy

The Vivaldi music meant she was in a good mood. He set his beer down.

"We have enough money to go this summer."

"I don't want to go to Italy."

"Why not?"

"Because, I'm pregnant."

A bead of moisture ran down the amber glass and landed in a tiny puddle.

"Coaster," she said.

Writing tip

Do not dispense your commas with a salt shaker. Place them with care and purpose. A poorly placed comma, or the lack of one, can change everything. "Let's eat Grandma!"

—The Editors

I miss cursive and I miss knowing people by their handwriting. The typed word is useful, though. This contest is an example. The National ePrescribing Patient Safety Initiative reduced medical injuries caused by sloppy handwriting by 90%. Also good. Even still, as school ends, here's a plea to not give up on penmanship.

Write a 53-word story about **a script**

Breaking Good News
by Chris Tattersall

The smile on his face told his anxious wife that all was okay.

"It was all very positive—don't worry," he said.

"So what's the prescription for?" she asked.

"Dunno, didn't say."

She examined her husband's prescription closer. "This is powerful stuff, love. When you say 'positive,' what exactly did the doctor say?"

Writing tip
Keep a journal of ambiguous words, puns, funny/odd wordplay that you come across in everyday life. This story evolved from a conversation with a co-worker over a negative test when someone said, "Oh, that's positive." Also, leave the end unsaid; give the reader some intellectual credit, which also helps in showing, not telling. —Chris Tattersall

Prompt for
July 2023

This month's contest will again run from the first until the fifteenth. Since it's July, that means from Creative Ice Cream Flavors Day until Cow Appreciation Day. Growing up, I believed that chocolate milk came from chocolate cows, so if it's your choice, don't forget to appreciate your local avocado-maple-bacon-caramel-sea-salt cow this month!

Write a 53-word story about **a combination**

Rice & Ice
by Kane Williams

As he opened the lid, a billowing cloud of steam burst from the rice cooker. He lowered in a spoon and pushed around the sticky, soggy grains. "Honey, did you make congee?"

"No." Her voice came from the bedroom.

"How much water did you add?"

"How thin is the ice you're standing on?"

Writing tip
The initial brainstorming of ideas is the most crucial step. It's not one to be rushed. Explore the possibilities of the prompt. What resonates with you? What can you bring to the piece (e.g., something unique, fresh, relatable, surprising through a twist, etc.)? What emotion do you want to evoke in the reader? —Kane Williams

Prompt for
August 2023

This month in 1587 Elenora and Ananias Dare welcomed their daughter, Virginia, as the first child born to English parents on American soil. Little is known about the lives of these teenage parents, especially their fate as a family of three in the Lost Colony. There are still those, though, continuing to look.

Write a 53-word story about a **search**

This Living Hand
by Gary Thomson

The child spreads attentive fingers over the rock face, pinching the charcoal foreleg of a galloping bison. His mother inhales, spits a cloud of reddish paint toward his hand. He strokes the made silhouette, laughter echoing into cavern chambers, resounding twenty thousand years later when French archaeologists scan headlamps over the lucid outline.

Writing tip

Story is essential to culture, to transmitting historical knowledge that encourages human survival, both physical and emotional. Collective stories often expand over centuries. Microfiction, in reverse, takes a story and boils it down to the very few bits and pieces needed to capture the author's intent. In order to write a successful micro, fight the instinct to expand. —Tara Lynn Masih, editor of *The Rose Metal Press Field Guide to Writing Flash Fiction*

October 2023

Before Lewis Carroll wrote "Jabberywocky," he must have looked at the words *chuckle* and *snort*, decided he needed both where only one would do, and created *chortle*. For Halloween I'll be a wolf or superhero, but still need to just be Dad, walking the streets in portmanteau as a little bit of both.

Write a 53-word story about **a blend**

Innovation
by Magdalena Naziemiec

"Ta-da!" he cried.

Something like a wagon wheel hung from the ceiling. Lightbulbs dotted the perimeter, and a fern was cradled in the center, its long fronds bowing down toward the floor.

"Impressive," she mused. "Chandelier with a plant . . . I suppose, a plantchelier?"

His face fell. "Oh. I was calling it a plamp."

Writing tip
Every sentence must do one of two things—reveal character or advance the action. —Kurt Vonnegut, Jr.

Prompt for
November 2023

We're told its good luck to break one on stage, but any other time is bad. It's good to have one in a debate, but let's enjoy a snack and share a few while I tell you about my trip; oh yeah, and the trip that put a hole in one of mine.

Write a 53-word story about **a leg**

Autumn Heir
by Keith Padraic

My father carves the turkey, a leg each for the two of us—wings for my younger sisters. He slices the breast, making even medallions as he progresses inward. With hands trembling from the chemotherapy, he asks if I'm paying attention. I nod, listening like never before, knowing I'll be carving next year.

Writing tip

When in doubt, start with the concrete (versus the abstract); find the change, even small, in the story; consider a title that does *work* for the story—that adds to the piece or helps the reader enter the piece. —Shuly Xóchitl Cawood, author of *What the Fortune Teller Would Have Said*

In the heart of winter's domain, the winter solstice marks the year's turning point. Day surrenders to night, a symphony of shadows dancing under the starry expanse. Yet, amidst the hushed tranquility, a promise stirs—the sun's gentle ascent, beckoning forth the promise of spring's renewal. The preceding sentences were written by AI.

Write a 53-word story about **a code**

Chocolate
by Audrey Brown

I broke their code ages ago; they aren't as subtle as they think they are. Her raised eyebrow means "Don't eat one, they're for later." His smirk means "But you know you love me." A yelp, muffled laughter, he walks away triumphant, she smiles and wipes chocolate off her lips. I smile too.

Writing tip

Pick one strong emotion, the kind that sizzles, burns, or fizzes out in an instant. That's your story's heart. Hone in on a specific moment that could generate this big emotion—and then dive into the details. Let readers see, taste, touch, hear, or smell this blink-and-you'll-miss-it feeling. And then leave them craving more. —Hayley Igarashi, "Ship Seeking Ship," (August 2021)

At midnight local time, everyone in the USA crossed over into a new year. In China, the new year begins somewhere between January 21 and February 20. Regardless of your calendar, at some point a new year arrives, and with it, many hope for a better life, a fresh start, peace for all.

Write a 53-word story about **a beginning**

Ciao Is Two Words
by Leeron Carmi

I've only just started to sort the trash properly and now I feel a pressure to speak the language I've struggled with for the past two years. The cab driver is waiting and my luggage is full, but I squeeze in my landlady's rusted moka pot anyways, even though I don't drink coffee.

Writing Tip
What dwells between the lines is essential in very short fiction. That which is "unsaid" but implied is integral. It hints of a broader, more nuanced sense of what's at stake; what a reader can imagine existing beyond a small word count, making the borders permeable, more expansive. Suggestive details are paramount in partnering with the reader's imagination, and in creating a sense of resonance and deeper understanding well after the last word is read.
—Robert Scotellaro, co-editor of *New Micro:
Exceptionally Short Fiction* (W.W. Norton)

Prompt for
April 2024

Of the many collective nouns used for animals—crash, shrewdness, conspiracy, business, murder, prickle, fever, shiver, and galaxy, to name a few—one obvious one seems to be missing. Humans use it often in unifying places: marriages, people, music, colors and striations, even machinery, and anything else we need just a bit tighter.

Write a 53-word story about **a band**

At Long Last
by Allison Winstead

He stared from the summit down the steep and narrow descent. A delicious kind of fear fluttered in his stomach as he prepared to take his place among the previous, brave conquerors of Poseidon's Peak.

Finally, at forty-eight inches tall, he had earned his right to the red wristband at the water park.

Writing Tip
When writing your 53-word story, look up the prompt in a dictionary and see how many definitions you find. This could point you in an interesting direction for your story. For example, the word "run" has 645 definitions, and that's only if you use *run* as a verb. —The Editors

Contributor 53-Word Biographies

Anne Anthony credits her steady diet of comic books for her ardent belief in superpowers. *Cleaver Magazine* nominated her micro-fiction, "It's a Mother Thing," for Best Microfiction 2024. She is the art director for *Does It Have Pockets* literary journal. She lives and writes in Carrboro, North Carolina. Find more writing here: linktr.ee/anchalastudio. ("Might Get Lucky," March 2018)

Riddhishrree Badhan was a high school student when she wrote her story. She is now at Washington University in St. Louis, studying molecular biology and biochemistry. She has always loved creative writing, her favorite part of the process being the meticulous crafting of characters. Her other interests include astronomy, board games, and elephants. ("Lazy Sunday," August 2020)

Elizabeth Barton (1974-2022) wrote nearly continually upon learning the alphabet until the last day she could wield a pen or keyboard. She kept her writing muscles lithe and toned as a professional medical writer and a prolific creator of fiction. She completed two novels and her works appeared in multiple anthologies and online publications. **Editors' note:** We thank Elizabeth's husband, Ian, for granting us permission to reprint Elizabeth's story. All of us at Press 53 send condolences to Elizabeth's family and friends. ("Endurance," February 2020)

A geek at heart, **Deborah Block-Schwenk** has had a handful of stories published under a pen name with small presses in a variety of genres (science fiction, fantasy, romance). She's been writing as long as she can remember. Deborah lives in Boston with her husband and four cats, two of whom are black. ("Ergot," March 2023)

Jane Laube Boch's fiction and short-form memoir have been featured on Silver Birch Press and in the Wordrunner e-chapbook *Love*. Streaming Marvel and *Star Trek* movies gets her through times of turmoil—and boosts her spirits while she continues to query her novel manuscript. Find her on Instagram @janelaubeboch and online at janelaubeboch.com ("Open Road," June 2015)

Audrey Brown is a Biology PhD student from Salt Lake City, Utah. While she writes mostly about science, she is eager to stretch her creative muscles by writing short stories and poetry (and maybe a novel one day). She survives the cold winter months curled up with hot chocolate and a good book. ("Chocolate," December 2023)

Sandra Burley lives near, but not near enough, the beach in South Carolina where she raises cats, cacti and a very small amount of cane. Sandra has been published in a collection of memoirs. She is currently at work on a novel and short stories about nightlife in Charleston in the last century. ("Equine Knocks," September 2021)

While **Leeron Carmi** studies architecture in Milan, Italy, writing has become her favorite form of procrastination. She enjoys telling stories through any medium she can, from walls to words, and has a soft spot for bad puns, beautiful hikes, and impromptu train travels. People are her inspiration, and she tries to listen closely. ("Ciao Is Two Words," January 2024)

Annie Dodson enjoys observing nature in the Florida Panhandle with her husband Scott and their dog Pete. She works as an engineer for a global plastics company by day and writes fiction by night. She is a member of the Pensacola Writing and Critique Group. This is her first published work of fiction. ("Low Tide," June 2018)

Sara Elizabeth (Elle) Dowd is a Spanish interpreter who side hustles as an adjunct professor. She lives in New York where she does volunteer cat fostering. You might find her playing War at the casino (which isn't *really* considered gambling) when she's not occupied perfecting her mom's quiche recipe or practicing hot yoga. ("Please Follow Proper Courtroom Etiquette," February 2022)

H.T. Grossen lives and writes beneath the long evening shadow of the Rocky Mountains in Pueblo, Colorado, with his magical wife, pulchritudinous daughters, and several animals of varying levels of intelligence. He pens fiction of all genres and teaches high school writing and literature. His first book of poetry is out now. htgrossen. com ("Dusk," April 2022)

Poet, writer, and adjunct professor of English, **Greg Hill** lives in West Hartford, Connecticut. His work has appeared in *Six Sentences*, *Otoliths*, *Visitant*, *Past Ten*, and elsewhere. He has an MFA in Writing from Vermont College of Fine Arts. He and his wife enjoy the struggle of raising three determined feminists. Twitter: @PrimeArepo ("The Buzz about the Wedding," July 2021)

Sheri Holden-Peck has been a law enforcement dispatcher, radio disc jockey, and voice-over artist. An avid lover of SciFi and Fantasy, she now writes her own, joining the stories she's written for her granddaughters. She's looking forward to trying her hand at stand-up comedy, gaining inspiration from kids, kittens and kooks calling 9-1-1. ("Ineptias Verba," December 2022)

Jordan Hua is a thirteen-year-old from British Columbia. She likes the idea of becoming a future writer, but honestly has no idea what she wants to do when she gets older. Apart from doing too much schoolwork, she usually spends her time reading. Other passions include pottery, piano, and clearly, eating sourdough bread. ("Sourdough," October 2022)

Raised in Alabama hill country, **Laura Hunter** lives "out in the country." She's published fiction, poetry, and free-lance articles. Her collection of stories, *Southern Voices*, and an Appalachian novel, *Beloved Mother*, are major award-winners. Hunter's recent novel, *Summer of No Rain*, is based on eugenics practiced in Alabama during the mid-twentieth century. ("Nine O'Clock Evening News," November 2016)

Hayley Igarashi is a full-time writer, part-time kayaker, and one-time trumpet player. She started her editorial career in Silicon Valley, but has since adapted quite well to remote work life and is never, ever going back. She now lives and writes near a lake in Maryland with her husband, young son, and dog. ("Ship Seeking Ship," August 2021)

Rachel Jager lives with her husband and three children in New Jersey, where she enjoys trying new recipes and singing songs from the 90s. Contrary to popular belief, she did not become a freelance writer just to have an excuse to drink endless amounts of coffee (but it is definitely her favorite perk). ("What She's Having," February 2021)

Zoë Jones is an aspiring writer living with her muse-turned-fiancé in California. When not composing lengthy emails for work, she enjoys experimenting with creative fiction. As a lover of both daydreams and nightmares, she is most interested in exploring that which keeps us up at night and picks loose our tightly knotted emotions. ("Lucky," September 2022)

Carrie Keyes is a former attorney and freelance writer from Coronado, California. Her manuscripts feature contemporary global issues with a faint rhythmic style, clandestine undertones, and flecks of plausible magic. Currently, she's enjoying writing Hollywood pitches, aligning herself with a talent manager, actors, and film producers to bring remarkable hidden histories to light. ("Leaving Kyiv," July 2022)

Audrey Lindsay left Oxford University with a degree in English Literature, then gained an acting diploma from a now-defunct drama school. After a varied career in entertainment, venue management and local government, she now works part-time in a prison while acting and writing on the side. Audrey lives in London with her husband. ("I Can Do It with My Eyes Shut," June 2021)

Laura Ruth Loomis authored two science fiction comedies, *The Cosmic Turkey* and *The Star-Crossed Pelican*. Her fiction and nonfiction have appeared in *The Saturday Evening Post*, *Writer's Digest*, *On the Premises*, and elsewhere. By day, Laura is a social worker, living in Northern California with her wife and a ridiculous number of pets. ("Hailstones," April 2018)

Madeleine McDonald finds Yorkshire's windswept beaches the best place to think. As a former précis-writer, she enjoys the challenge of squeezing big ideas into few words. Her short stories have been broadcast on BBC radio, and published in anthologies. Her poem on modern slavery won second prize for the 2023 Anita McAndrews Award. ("He Never Asked Me What I Wanted," November 2022)

Sue McMillan lives in Boise, Idaho with her husband and dog. She practiced law for a living, sneaking in writing catch-as-catch-can. In retirement her most knotty decisions are whether to ski, mountain bike, hike, write or read. Asked if she misses practicing law, she'll respond *res ipsa loquitur* while raising her wine glass. ("Walk a Mile," February 2023)

Nina Miller is a physician and fencer who started writing during the pandemic. Her work appears in the *Flash Flood Journal*, *Bright Flash Literary Review*, *50 Give or Take*, and *101 Words*. While she loves fish and chips, her brother, sister-in-law, and rambunctious twin nephews inspired this moment. Read more work at ninamillerwrites.com ("Craving for Two," January 2022)

Jill Mills, a ballistic engineer turned mother of two, took up writing during the pandemic to help keep her head on straight. Originally from the land of summer, sunny Arizona, she now enjoys the full array of seasons in Maryland. There, with her family and friends, she delves into many hobbies, writing included. ("Don't Mess with Dewey," March 2022)

Jo Mularczyk has stories and poems published within Australia, US and UK. She writes in diverse genres for adults and children, and is a Littlescribe co-author. A highlight was having a poem alongside Shakespeare, Lewis Carroll and Lord Tennyson in a Bloomsbury children's collection. She lives in Australia with her husband and children. ("The Signs," December 2020)

Amanda Murphy is a self-proclaimed coffee addict with a lifelong love of stories and writing. She is an extroverted introvert with enough hobbies to keep every day interesting. Most of all, she just enjoys being in the company of her dog and cats. Amanda hopes to continue exploring new areas with her writing. ("The End of the World as We Know It," May 2023)

Magdalena Naziemiec is excited to return to writing fiction after spending months writing and revising her dissertation. Besides writing, she enjoys baking, a hot cup of tea, and curling up with a good mystery. She lives in the Chicago area with her boyfriend and dreams about the day they finally get a corgi. ("Innovation," October 2023)

Janette Ostle lives in Wigton, Cumbria, UK. She enjoys walking and often finds inspiration from thoughts which occur whilst outdoors. Prone to occasional tongue-tied moments, she finds expressing herself on paper easier, as well as cathartic. She's had poems and prose published in various anthologies and is delighted to be November's contest winner. ("Unforgettable," November 2021)

Keith Padraic lives in Rhode Island where he works as a graphic designer and content editor. He spends much of his free time writing, exploring themes such as the modern domestic drama, consumerism, and the juxtaposition of traditionalism versus neoteric technologies. Keith's stories are often inspired by his personal experiences and family history. ("Final Request," October 2021, and "Autumn Heir," November 2023)

Jane T. Pait, a Language Arts teacher for over fifty years, loves telling her nine grandchildren stories in which they are the main characters. This story stars her triplet granddaughters who are now sixteen. Jane lives in North Carolina in a small village, White Oak. She is married to her high school sweetheart. ("Alone," November 2019)

Angel Pritts lives in Pennsylvania with her husband and four children. She enjoys writing novels and short stories. She hopes to return to community theatre in the near future. Angel's lifelong dream is to appear on a game show, preferably *Jeopardy!*. In her spare time, she looks at cat pictures on the internet. ("What Defines You," May 2021)

Amanda Van Regenmorter is a chemical engineer, community theatre enthusiast, and Unitarian Universalist who recently traded bleak gray winters in the mitten state for a home in the sunny southwest. Some of her favorite people include her lovely husband and children and her writing group who still let her video chat into meetings. ("Round and Round," January 2023)

Brian Rosten is a science teacher in Urbana, Illinois. He writes in his free time when he's not roasting teenagers or wrangling small children. Brian's favorite books are *The Two Towers*, *Nightwatch*, and *Leviathan Wakes*. His favorite short story is "Brownies" by ZZ Packer. Brian edits *The Maul*, an obscure YA horror magazine. ("Guts," April 2019, and "Good Night," December 2019)

N.E. Rule attended MTU for communications and creative writing. When Covid hit, her creative side finally came out to play. Since then, she has been published online and in fifteen print anthologies. Her amazing publishers include Black Hare Press, Off Topic Publishing, and Press 53. "Premature Congratulations" was her first contest win. http://nerule. com ("Premature Congratulations," September 2020)

Scott B. Shepherd didn't convert to serious reading until later in life but has been writing since childhood. He now sees the symbiotic relationship between reading and writing and loves to do both. He has written in many forms and especially loves the challenge of word count restrictions to get his imagination going. ("Breakaway," January 2020)

Paul Adam Short is a writer and poet from Newcastle upon Tyne, England. He is currently working on his debut poetry pamphlet and a collection of short stories. When not writing, Paul enjoys countryside and coastal walks with his wife and their dog Brody, playing his saxophone and listening to old jazz records. ("That Awkward First Kiss," April 2021)

Jean-Luke Swanepoel was born in South Africa, and lives in California with his husband. Following publication in *Prime Number Magazine*, his work has appeared in *Lunch Ticket*, *CutBank*, and *Necessary Fiction*, among others. He is the author of *The Thing About Alice* (2020), and enjoys reading (especially Muriel Spark) in his spare time. ("Buy a Donkey," November 2020)

Chris Tattersall is a Health Service Research Manager and lives with his wife Hayley and Border Collie in Pembrokeshire, Wales. He is a self-confessed flash fiction addict with some publication and competition success. A recent obsession of his being writing Novella-In-Flash. He also hosts his own flash fiction website with a free competition. ("Breaking Good News," June 2023)

Kristin Tenor finds inspiration in life's quiet details and believes in their power to illuminate the extraordinary. Her work has appeared in *Wigleaf*, *X-R-A-Y*, *Bending Genres*, *Unbroken*, and elsewhere. Her flash fiction has also been nominated for various awards, including the Pushcart Prize and longlisted in Wigleaf's Top 50. Read more at www.kristintenor.com ("And All the Heavens Are in Disarray," July 2020)

Joanna Thomas is both visual artist and poet, residing in Ellensburg, Washington. She is the author of the chapbooks *blue•bird (bloo-burd)* (Milk & Cake Press, 2021) and *[ache] [blur] [cut]: sonnets* (Open Country Press, 2023). She wrote this story in her head while stirring bechamel sauce over medium heat until bubbles rose. ("How Amelia Earhart Comes to Understand Gravitational Pull," June 2017)

Gary Thomson lives in southern Ontario. His abiding interest in ancestry extends from the earliest human migrations out of Africa, to the Clovis peoples' settlements in the Americas. This narrative was inspired by the ancient cave art at Lascaux II, and a reminder of the primal human need to say, "I was here." ("This Living Hand," August 2023)

Born in New Jersey in Eisenhower times, **Mike Tuohy** moved to Georgia in 1965 and has sopped up Southern culture ever since. A professional geologist working the environmental consulting rackets by day, he chronicles the preposterous via stories disguised as fiction by night. Free samples are available at his website, bunker93a.com (Chronicles page). **Editors' note:** While putting together this anthology, we learned that Mike Tuohy died on March 7, 2021, at the age of 67. Mike used to travel from Georgia to North Carolina with his wife Sally for Press 53's annual Wine & Words Fest. He was a joy to be around. Seeing Mike's obituary photo with him wearing his Press 53 ball cap brought us a smile and broke our hearts just a little more. Thank you, Sally, for granting us permission to reprint Mike's stories. ("Ancestry," December 2015, and "Taking the Fall," September 2018)

Beverley Ward writes a bit of everything and runs a lot of workshops from her home town of Sheffield where she lives with her two children and two cats. She's the owner of The Writers Workshop, which helps writers make their dreams come true. This is a little dream come true for her. ("The Last Word," August 2022)

Emily West is a former French translator with an enduring love of language and nuanced expression. She is currently retooling her writing for academic audiences as a PhD student investigating psychological reactance and health communication strategies. She writes from Austin, Texas, where she lives with her husband Will, daughter Margot, and Bernedoodle Remy. ("Nuptials," August 2018)

Kane Williams believes that the pen is mightier than the sword (and asks that you kindly don't tell Excalibur he said that). Currently, he is working on the third draft of his fast-paced high fantasy novel. Kane previously wrote nonfiction and was published by Thomson Reuters. His website hosts his flash fiction blog. ("Rice & Ice," July 2023)

Allison Winstead is a financial professional from rural Mississippi who spends an embarrassing amount of time daydreaming, mostly about being interviewed by *60 Minutes* for writing the next great American novel. She loves the written word in all its forms, baking, and sharing a home with daughter (Reagan), husband (Shey), and furbaby (Nola). ("At Long Last," April 2024)

Theresa Wyatt follows the tug of history, eulogy, art, and therapeutic medical narratives in her writing. She is the author of *The Beautiful Transport*, a chapbook, (Moonstone Press) and *Hurled Into Gettysburg* (BlazeVox Books). Her work has appeared in *New Flash Fiction Review*, *Spillway*, *The Ekphrastic Review*, *The Healing Muse*, and *The Phare*. ("Gettysburg, July, 1863," August 2016)

Ada Young was in seventh grade when she wrote "Underground Fugitive." Now, as an eleventh grader in Thibodaux, Louisiana, Ada still adores the creative life. She enjoys her pottery studio, countless school clubs, and a newfound love for tennis. Almost every summer, Ada travels to exciting places and collects inspiration for her writings. ("Underground Fugitive," March 2021)

Editor 53-Word Biographies

Christopher Forrest lives in Winston-Salem, North Carolina, with his wife and three young children. After a near-decade career in finance, Chris earned his MFA in Creative Writing from Queens University of Charlotte. Outside of writing and Press 53, Christopher stays busy with family life and training for triathlon. He prefers vinegar-based BBQ sauce.

Claire Foxx is a North Carolina-based editor, writer, and lifelong book enthusiast. She holds degrees in Creative Writing and English Literature and knows either too much or just enough about commas, depending on who you ask. Her phone's notes app contains multitudes, and local coffee shop staff know her on a first-name basis.

Ella Watson is a Winston-Salem native and has been reading and writing since she first learned how to decipher scribbles. If you ask her family, her greatest strength is making her locally famous cinnamon chocolate chip cookies. She is an avid traveler and has a talent for naming things (like her cat, Squid).

Kevin Morgan Watson founded Press 53 in October 2005. His plan was to publish writing he loved and then set out to find readers who agreed with him. Today, Press 53 has published nearly three hundred titles by writers in thirty-seven U.S. states, with readers around the world. Kevin's lucky number is 53.

www.ingramcontent.com/pod-product-compliance
Lightning Source LLC
Chambersburg PA
CBHW052014240626
47153CB00008B/2873
9781950413812